for Bill and Phyllis

This special edition was printed in 2011 for Kohl's Department Stores, Inc.
(for distribution on behalf of Kohl's Cares, LLC, its wholly owned subsidiary)
by Philomel Books, a division of Penguin Young Readers Group.

Kohl's
978-0-399-25571-7
123386
09/11 – 02/12

Library of Congress Cataloging-in-Publication Data
Carle, Eric. The very busy spider.
    Summary: The farm animals try to divert a busy little spider from spinning her web,
but she persists and produces a thing of both beauty and usefulness. The pictures may be felt as well as seen.
1. Toy and movable books—Specimens. [1. Spiders—Fiction. 2. Spider webs—Fiction.
3. Domestic animals—Fiction. 4. Toy and movable books] 1. Title.
PZ7.C21476Ve 1985 [E] 84-5907
This edition ISBN 978-0-399-25571-7
10 9 8 7 6 5 4 3 2 1

Eric Carle

The Very Busy Spider

Philomel Books
New York

Early one morning the wind blew a spider across the field.
A thin, silky thread trailed from her body.
The spider landed on a fence post near a farm yard . . .

and began to spin a web with her silky thread.

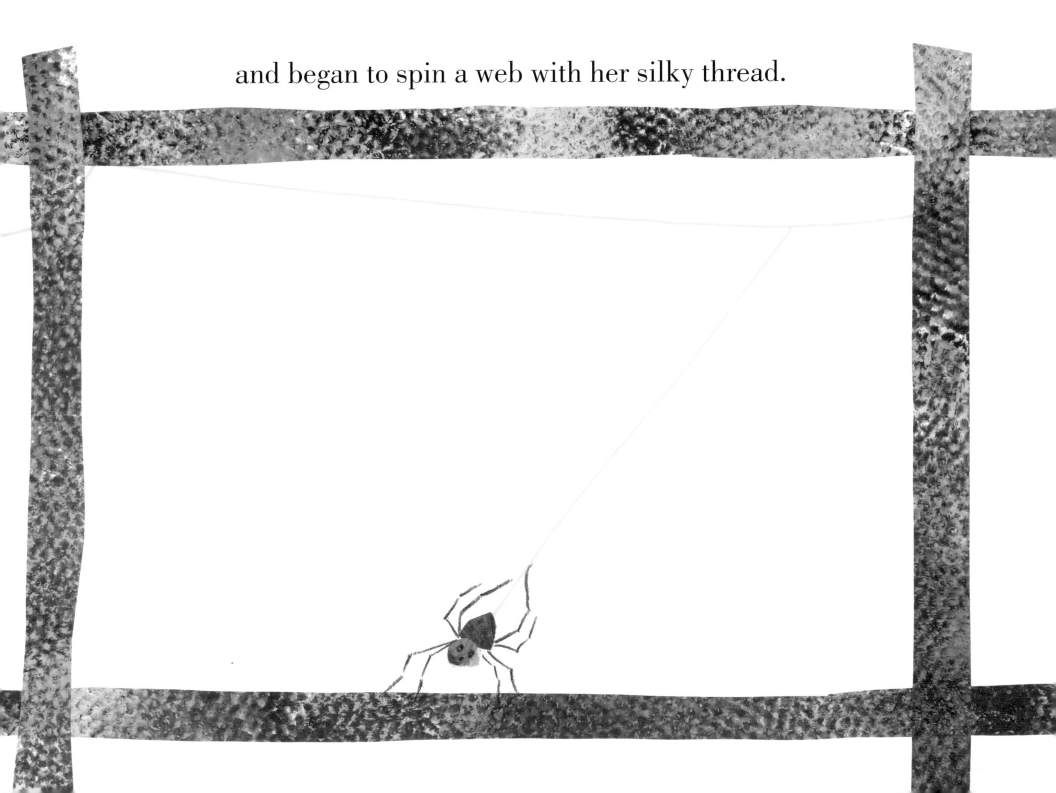

"Neigh! Neigh!" said the horse. "Want to go for a ride?"

The spider didn't answer. She was very busy spinning her web.

"Moo! Moo!" said the cow. "Want to eat some grass?"

The spider didn't answer. She was very busy spinning her web.

"Baa! Baa!" bleated the sheep. "Want to run in the meadow?"

The spider didn't answer. She was very busy spinning her web.

"Maa! Maa!" said the goat. "Want to jump on the rocks?"

The spider didn't answer. She was very busy spinning her web.

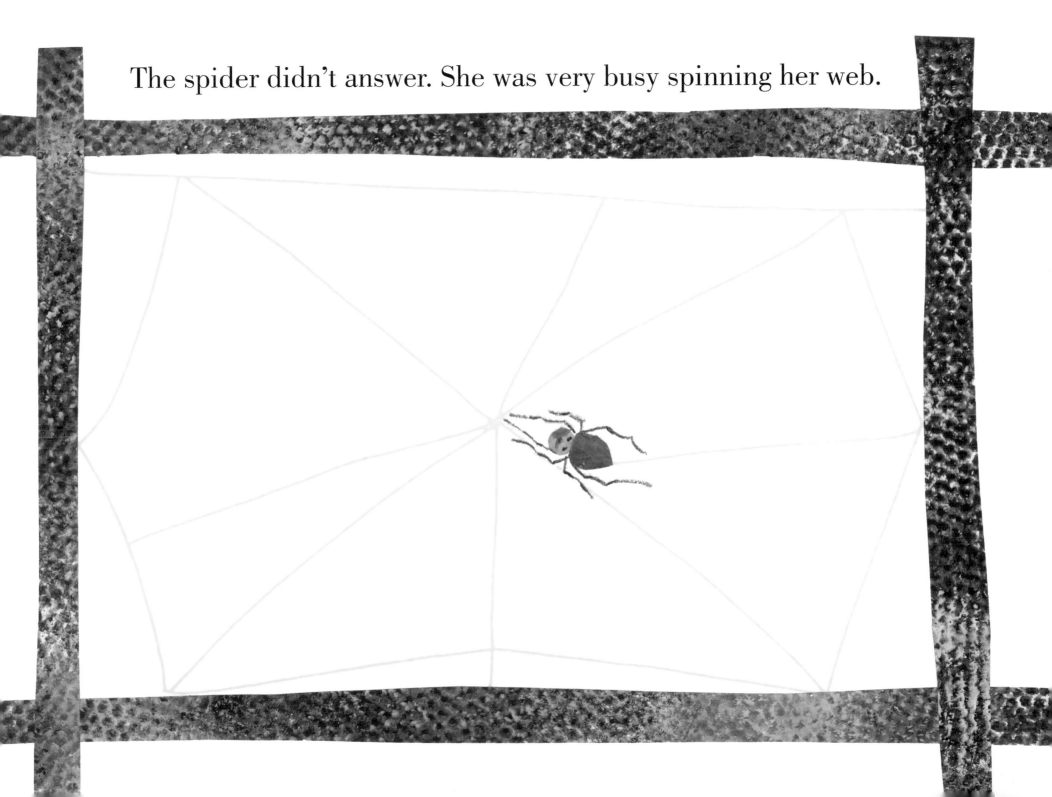

"Oink! Oink!" grunted the pig. "Want to roll in the mud?"

The spider didn't answer. She was very busy spinning her web.

"Woof! Woof!" barked the dog. "Want to chase a cat?"

The spider didn't answer. She was very busy spinning her web.

"Meow! Meow!" cried the cat. "Want to take a nap?"

The spider didn't answer. She was very busy spinning her web.

"Quack! Quack!" called the duck. "Want to go for a swim?"

The spider didn't answer. She had now finished her web.

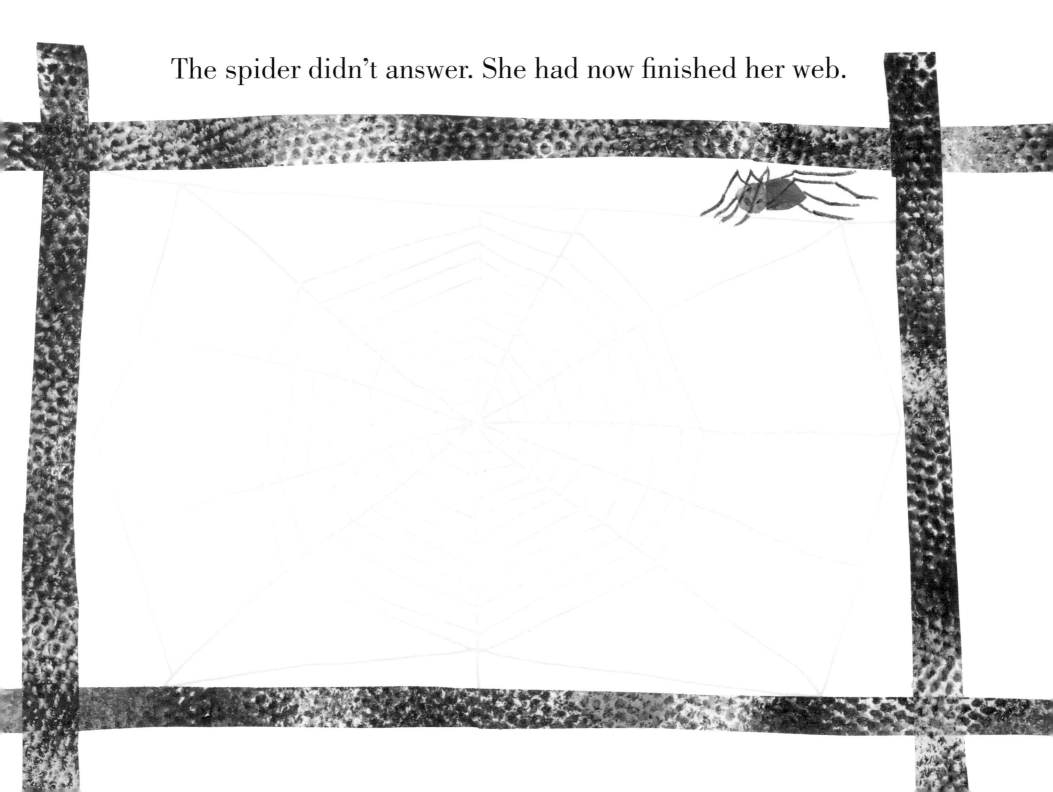

"Cock-a-doodle do!" crowed the rooster. "Want to catch a pesty fly?"

And the spider caught the fly in her web . . . just like that!

"Whoo? Whoo?"
asked the owl.
"Who built this
beautiful web?"
The spider
didn't answer.
She had
fallen asleep.

It had been
a very, very
busy day.